my Head is full of colors

Catherine Friend • Illustrated by Kiki

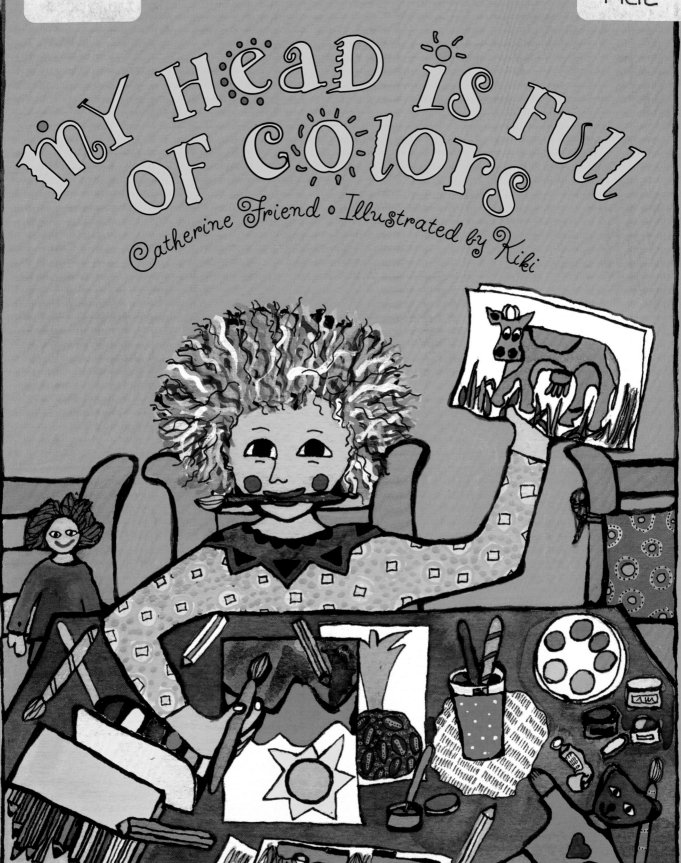

HYPERION BOOKS FOR CHILDREN • NEW YORK

One morning Maria woke up and looked in the mirror. "Oh my!" she said. Instead of her usual brown spiky hair, her hair was fire red and sky blue and emerald green and lemon yellow and cotton candy pink!

Maria raced down the hall. "Look, Mom, my head is full of colors!"

"Good heavens!" she cried. "You've slept on a rainbow!"

For the next few days, Maria colored and painted like she had never done before. She painted pink mountains and blue meadows and yellow rivers and red cows.

Her mother looked over her shoulder as she was painting one night. "Maria, you're using such beautiful colors."

"Of course, Mom," Maria replied. "My head is full of colors."

The next morning Maria woke up and looked in the mirror. "Oh dear!" she said. Instead of brilliant streaks of rainbow colors running through her hair, there were hundreds of books! Little books and big books, open books and closed books, books with colorful pictures, and books with many words.

Maria scampered down the hall. "Look, Mom, my head is full of books!"

"My goodness," her mother said. "Perhaps I could borrow one to read."

For the next few days, Maria read and thought like she had never done before. She read about lions in Africa and artists in Paris and caribou in Canada. She read about growing pumpkins and making piñatas and flying spaceships to the moon.

Her mother overheard Maria telling a friend about how spiders spin their webs. "Maria, you have learned a lot of interesting facts about spiders."

"Of course, Mom," Maria replied. "My head is full of books."

A few days later Maria woke up and looked in the mirror. "Yikes!" she said. Instead of quiet books stacked in her hair, there were animals—live animals! Giraffes and dogs and monkeys and birds and elephants and turtles—screeching and barking and making all sorts of sounds.

Maria dashed down the hall. "Look, Mom, my head is full of animals!"

"My, my," her mother said. "We don't usually allow animals in the house, but I suppose we can just this once."

For the next few days, Maria attracted animals as if she were a zookeeper at feeding time. Birds followed Maria wherever she went. Cats jumped up into her lap whenever she sat down. Squirrels ran alongside her on the sidewalk.

Her mother watched her safely escort a turtle back to the pond. "Maria, you are so gentle and kind with animals."

"Of course, Mom," Maria replied. "My head is full of animals."

The following morning Maria woke up and looked in the mirror. "Wow!" she said. Instead of animals roaming through her hair, rows and rows of people smiled and waved to her in the mirror! Young people and old people, short people and tall people.

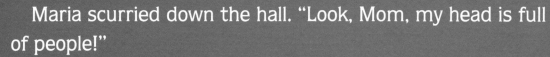

Maria scurried down the hall. "Look, Mom, my head is full of people!"

"Gracious me," her mother said. "Well, you had better ask them all to stay for breakfast."

For the next few days, Maria talked with everyone she and her mother met on their walks. She talked with young mothers about working and about babies. She talked with old men about the weather and about baseball. She talked with Mrs. Webster, the woman living next door, about what life was like when she was Maria's age.

"That was very nice of you to spend time talking with Mrs. Webster. She gets lonely sometimes," Maria's mother said. "You certainly have a way with people."

"Of course, Mom," Maria replied. "My head is full of people."

Then one morning Maria woke up and looked in the mirror and said…nothing…because there was nothing in her hair! No colors, no books, no animals, no people. Just plain brown spikes.

Maria shuffled down the hall, sobbing. "Mom," she whispered. "My head is empty. There's nothing there." She threw herself into her mother's arms.

Maria's mother held her by the shoulders and looked at her.
"No, dear, there must be something wrong with your mirror.

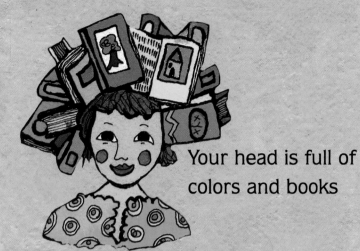

Your head is full of colors and books

and hippopotamuses

and dancers.

There's a little girl on a pony reading a book.

And a man with two llamas by his side.

And a set of bright red encyclopedias. It's amazing how all that fits in your head!"

Maria ran back to her mirror and looked at herself very hard. She frowned and she squinted and she wrinkled up her nose.

"All I see is my old brown hair," she said to the mirror. "But then…I still like bright colors…and books…and animals…and people. Hmmm."

Maria skipped down the hall with her head held high.
"Look, Mom, my head is full of me!"

103910

Ja
Friend
My head is full of colors

2/95   15.95